D0997748

Petal Parade

ROSIE BANKS

This is the Secret Kingdom

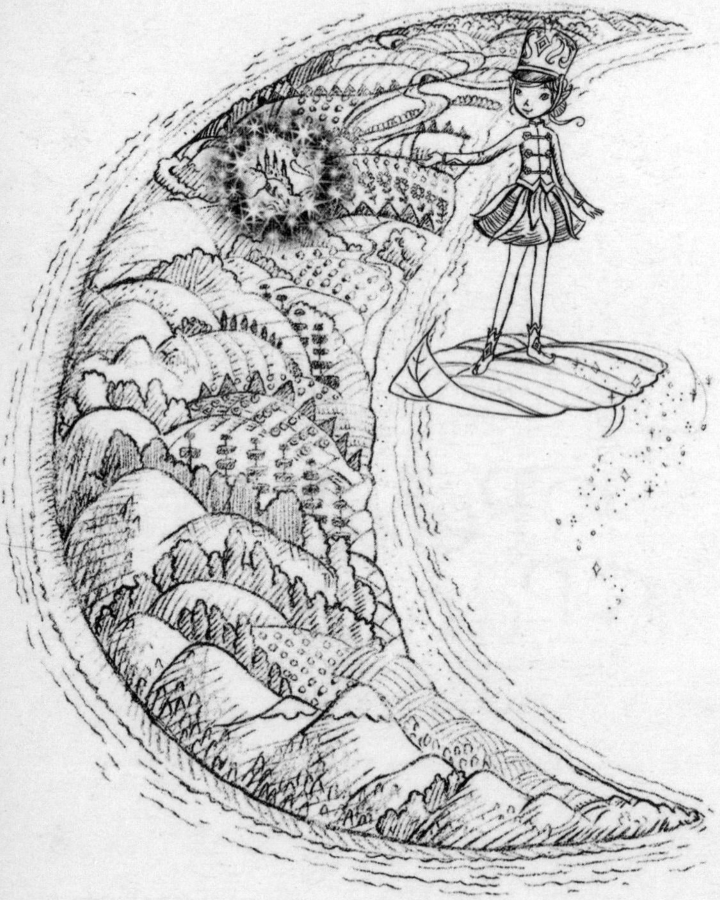

The Secret Garden

Book One

Contents

A Garden Riddle

Butterflies danced from flower to flower in the sunshine and birds sang in the trees. It was a beautiful summer's day and Jasmine Smith was helping her grandmother – Nani – in their garden.

Best of all, her two friends, Summer Hammond and Ellie Macdonald, were helping as well!

Nani, who lived with Jasmine and her mum, was trimming some roses while the girls planted flowers in pots.

"I love gardening!" said Summer, pushing her blonde bunches back over her shoulder as she watched a ladybird walk across a plant pot.

"Me too," said Jasmine. "I love the smell of the flowers and the earth."

Ellie had taken a little break from planting and was drawing one of Nani's garden gnomes in her sketchbook. All

the little plastic gnomes had a red hat, white beard and rosy cheeks. Some were fishing, others were sweeping or pushing wheelbarrows.

"These gnomes are so cute," Ellie said. She grinned and picked up the one she was drawing. "You know what he's saying?" she asked the others.

"What?" replied Summer.

"There's no place like gnome!"

Summer and Jasmine giggled.

Jasmine dusted her gloves off. "Why don't you tell the plants a story, Summer? It might help them to grow."

Nani chuckled as she walked past them with a watering can. "I'm not sure stories help plants grow," she said. "What they need is sunshine and water, and what you girls need is your lunch. Why don't

I go and get some food ready while you finish off here?"

"Thanks, Nani," said Jasmine as her grandmother went inside.

"I know Nani says that plants don't need stories to grow," Ellie whispered, "but they do in the Secret Kingdom!"

The three girls all shared a smile. They had an amazing secret. They looked after a magical box that could whisk them away to an amazing land called the Secret Kingdom. All sorts of wonderful creatures like mermaids and unicorns, elves and brownies lived there, all ruled by a jolly king named King Merry.

"Do you remember the time we went to Fairytale Forest?" asked Summer. "And saw books growing on trees!"

Jasmine nodded. "It was brilliant!"

"Oh, I do love the Secret Kingdom!" Ellie said, her green eyes shining. "I hope we go there again soon. It's been ages since King Merry last asked us to visit."

"We could look at the Magic Box now and see if there's a message for us," said Summer hopefully.

"Good idea," said Jasmine. "It's up on my desk in my bedroom." Jasmine didn't have nosy little brothers or sisters, so she didn't have to be as careful as Ellie and Summer when it was her turn to look after the Magic Box.

The girls ran into the house. Jasmine stuck her head into the kitchen, where her grandmother was busy getting their lunch ready. "We're just going up to my room, Nani."

Ellie and Summer followed Jasmine into her bedroom. There was a bed with pretty netting over it and hot pink walls covered with posters of Jasmine's favourite dancers and singers. On a neat white desk sat the Magic Box – and it was shimmering with magical light!

"King Merry *has* sent us a message!" Ellie exclaimed.

"Quick! Let's see what it says," cried Summer excitedly.

The Magic Box had wooden sides carved with fantastic creatures and its mirrored lid was shining brightly. Words in swirly writing scrolled across the lid. Ellie read them out loud:

"The place you seek hides out of view,
With flowers, plants and a fountain, too!"

She frowned and looked at the others. "I wonder what *that* means?"

"We need the map to solve the riddle," said Jasmine.

The lid of the box opened and a map floated out of one of the compartments inside. It unfolded itself in front of the girls' noses. They leaned over the map eagerly and watched with delight as the pictures on it magically moved. There were lilac-coloured otters splashing in the sparkling waters of Sapphire Stream, fluffy snow bears tumbling through the pink snow near the Snow Bear Sanctuary, and pixies swooping around the turrets of the pixie flying school. Just looking at them made Jasmine tingle with excitement. The Secret Kingdom was such an incredible place!

"We need to find somewhere with flowers and plants," she said.

"It sounds like it might be a garden," said Summer.

"There are loads of gardens in the Secret Kingdom," said Ellie. "There are

gardens at the Enchanted Palace and at Starlight Manor. There are even gardens at Thunder Castle."

"I hope we don't have to go there," said Summer, shivering. Thunder Castle was the damp and creepy home of King Merry's horrible sister, Queen Malice. She lived there with her mean servants, the Storm Sprites.

"How about here?" Ellie said suddenly, pointing to a garden hidden in the centre of a wood. It had walls all around it covered with rambling roses. Inside it, she could see a fountain and lots of bright flowers spilling out of flowerbeds. "The Secret Garden," she said, reading the label beside the picture.

"I've never noticed that garden before," said Summer.

"Neither have I," said Jasmine. "But I bet it's the answer to the riddle!" They all put their hands on the Magic Box.

"The Secret Garden!" they chanted.

There was a bright golden flash and the

next second a ball of light zoomed out of the Magic Box. It turned a loop the loop and then, with a popping sound, changed into a tiny pixie standing on a leaf. She was wearing a dress made out of daisies and had a daisy chain headband holding back her short blonde hair.

"Trixi!" the girls cried together.

"Hello!" the little pixie replied in delight. "Are you ready to go to the Secret Garden?"

"Yes!" said Ellie. "Though we've never

noticed it on the map before."

Trixi giggled. "That's because it's secret, of course! Only a few people ever go there but King Merry really wants you to visit today."

"Why? Is something wrong? Is Queen Malice causing trouble again?" asked Summer anxiously. The girls had helped King Merry defeat the nasty queen lots of times before.

"No, everything's fine," said Trixi. "King Merry just thought you might like to see the Secret Garden and watch the Petal Parade with him."

"What's the Petal Parade?" Jasmine asked curiously.

Trixi's eyes twinkled. "You'll find out soon enough. Are you ready to go?"

"Oh, yes!" the girls cried, grabbing hold

of each others' hands.

Trixi tapped her ring and called out:

"The Secret Garden we wish to see,
Take Summer, Ellie, Jasmine and me!"

There was a bright flash of light and suddenly the girls felt themselves spinning and tumbling through the air. They were off to the Secret Garden!

An Unusual Gate

Ellie, Summer and Jasmine spun round and round until their feet came to rest down on some soft grass. As the sparkles cleared they saw that they were outside a walled garden with a shining golden gate. Pale pink flowers covered the garden's old brick walls, making the air smell sweet and wonderful.

"Mmm," said Jasmine, taking a deep breath. She touched her head. To her delight, her tiara was nestling in her long, dark hair. The girls' sparkling tiaras always appeared when they arrived in the Secret Kingdom. They showed everyone that the girls were Very Important Friends of King Merry.

"Look at our clothes!" said Ellie. As well as their tiaras, the girls were now wearing gardening smocks with pockets for tools. Ellie's smock had green-and-purple flowers on it, Summer's had a pattern of yellow flowers, and Jasmine's had pretty pink flowers. They also wore matching sparkly welly boots.

"Do you like them?" asked Trixi. "I thought you needed some clothes suitable for gardening."

"We've each got our favourite colours!" said Jasmine, doing a twirl.

"Now where's King Merry?" Trixi said, looking round. "He said that he would meet us here."

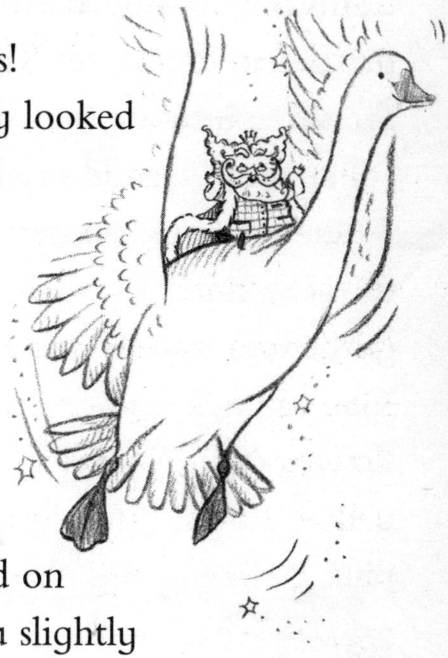

"My dear friends! Hellllooooo!" They looked up to the cloudless blue sky and saw the plump little king waving at them from the back of a giant white swan. His crown was perched on his white curls at a slightly wonky angle and he was wearing purple wellies that matched the gardening waistcoat under his royal cloak.

"Oh, daisies and dandelions!" he exclaimed as the swan landed safely. "It's simply splendid to see you again! He scrambled off the swan's back. "Thank you very much, Longfeather," he said, giving the swan a pat. "You may fly home now."

The swan bowed gracefully, then flapped its wings and flew back up into the blue sky.

The girls ran to hug King Merry.

"How are you all?" he said.

"We can't wait to go to the Secret Garden," said Ellie.

The king beamed. "Excellent! Usually only myself, Trixi and the Garden Gnomes who work here are allowed into the garden, but I really wanted to show it to my Very Important Friends."

Summer suddenly heard a faint rustling in the trees behind them. She glanced round. Maybe it was another wonderful animal like the giant swan? She went over to investigate, but there was nothing there. *I must have imagined it*, she thought, heading back to the others.

"Why do you keep the garden a secret, King Merry?" Jasmine asked the king.

King Merry's eyes twinkled. "Ah, well, every year my Garden Gnomes invent a new type of flower to be the highlight of the Petal Parade. They grow the flowers in the Secret Garden so that everyone gets a wonderful surprise when they see them for the first time."

"What's the Petal Parade?" Ellie asked, remembering that Trixi had mentioned it earlier on.

"It takes place in the middle of summer when floats decorated with flowers parade from the garden to the Enchanted Palace," King Merry explained.

"Everyone on the floats throws petals into the air," added Trixi. "The parade makes everyone watching it feel really happy, and their happiness creates a magic breeze. Then the breeze carries the petals all over the kingdom. New flowers grow wherever the petals land so the Secret Kingdom stays beautiful! And this year's Petal Parade is tomorrow afternoon!"

"Can we come?" asked Jasmine eagerly.

"You will be my guests of honour!" exclaimed King Merry, pushing his glasses up his nose. "But before the parade, you must see the Secret Garden and meet the Garden Gnomes. Come on, let's go in!"

Jasmine tried to open the gate. It was locked. She looked round at King Merry. "Have you got the key?"

He chuckled. "Everyone who wants to enter has their own key, my dear."

The girls looked at him in confusion.

"The gate will only let you in if you tell it a secret," he explained. "You must whisper your secret into the keyhole. Once you have each told it a secret, the gate will open for all of you. Try it!"

Just then, Summer heard another rustle

in the bushes behind her. She looked round and saw a flash of black among the green leaves. Maybe it was a blackbird? But there was no time to investigate. King Merry was waiting for them to tell the gate their secrets!

Jasmine went first. She bent down to the golden keyhole and hesitated. It was hard to think of a secret she hadn't told Ellie and Summer – she told her best friends nearly everything! But then she realised what she could say. She whispered, "I'm making a music playlist for the others with all our favourite songs."

Ellie went next. "I'm drawing special portraits for Summer and Jasmine for their birthdays," she whispered.

Finally, it was Summer's turn. "My mum and I are planning a surprise trip to take Ellie and Summer to Honeyvale Zoo," she said as quietly as she could.

The girls all looked at each other. Would their secrets work?

With a creak, the Secret Garden gate slowly started to open!

Amazing Flowers

The gate drew back to reveal the most beautiful garden Summer had ever seen. Flowerbeds were filled with blossoms of every colour and even more flowers spilled out of pots. Butterflies danced through the air, humming as they flitted from flower to flower. In the centre of the garden was a white marble fountain carved in the shape of a giant daffodil.

Water gushed out of its petals, falling into a glittering pool at the base.

"Look at the gnomes!" said Jasmine in delight. They looked just like her grandmother's garden gnomes – only they were real! They were hurrying about, pushing wheelbarrows, weeding, and filling up watering cans from the

fountain. They waved at the girls but kept on working busily.

King Merry clasped his hands in delight. "Oh, there's so much I want to show you. Come with me!"

The girls followed him into the garden with Trixi flying beside them on her leaf. The gate shut behind them with a creak.

"Over here are the Chameleon Carnations," said King Merry, leading them to some tall flowers with silvery petals. "They were the stars of the Petal Parade two years ago."

Jasmine went over for a closer look and the flowers immediately turned pink like her gardening smock. "Wow!" she gasped.

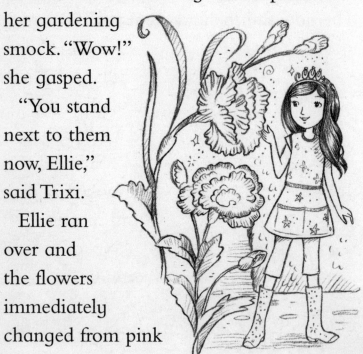

"You stand next to them now, Ellie," said Trixi.

Ellie ran over and the flowers immediately changed from pink to green-and-purple. "That's really cool!" she said with a grin.

"What about these roses?" said Summer, going over to a flowerbed full of pale pink roses. "Do these change colour too?" As she got close she caught a whiff of her favourite smell ever – vanilla. "They smell wonderful."

Ellie joined her. "Oh, yes! They smell of the seaside."

Summer looked at her in surprise. "No, of vanilla."

"You're both wrong,"

Jasmine said, sniffing a rose. "They smell of freshly baked bread. Mmm!"

King Merry chuckled. "They're Scent-sational Roses. They smell of whatever your favourite smell is. They were the highlight of the parade four years ago."

"And these are the Firework Tulips from last year's parade. They're my favourite," said Trixi, flying over to a patch of purple tulips. She touched one and its petals opened up and shot a stream of rainbow sparkles high into the sky.

"They're brilliant!" said Jasmine.

"Where are the flowers for this year's parade?" Summer asked eagerly.

"They're over this way," said King Merry. He led the girls to some tall plants that looked like sunflowers.

The girls examined them. The big yellow flowers didn't smell particularly sweet and they didn't change colour or seem to do anything magical.

"What do you think?" King Merry asked eagerly.

The girls exchanged confused looks. What was so special about them?

"They're very nice," said Ellie politely.

"They're very tall," put in Jasmine.

"And, er...very yellow," said Summer.

King Merry's eyes twinkled. "I think you'll find they're a lot more than that.

Watch this!" He clapped his hands. The flowers sprang to attention and burst into song, their petals opening and closing with each word they sang.

"Oh come to the
Petal Parade,
A day for fun
and play.
Oh come to the
Petal Parade,
Hip, hip, hip...
hooray!"

The girls gasped and Trixi turned her leaf in a happy loop-the-loop.

"Wow!" said Jasmine, for once lost for words. Flowers that could sing! They were amazing!

King Merry beamed. "I am so pleased with the songflowers. The gnomes tell me they are quite tricky to grow. Like most plants, they need lots of water and sunlight. But most importantly, they need happiness. Without it they wilt. Still," he said, his eyes twinkling, "that's not a problem in the Secret Garden. The gnomes are always very jolly."

"Just like you," Summer told him, giving him a hug.

The king looked delighted. "You're too kind, my dear. Now..." He pulled out a big gold pocket watch and checked it. "I should get back to the Enchanted Palace and put the finishing touches on the plan for my parade float. You girls are welcome to stay here and see if the gnomes would like some help. It is always very busy the day before the Petal Parade."

"We'd love to help them," Ellie said eagerly. The gnomes looked so sweet with their red hats, bushy beards and brightly coloured trousers.

Trixi tapped her ring and chanted:

"To the palace fly this merry king,
Please take him safely, pixie ring!"

Sparkles surrounded the king. "Byeee!" he called as he vanished into thin air.

"Let's see what we can do to help," said Trixi, flying over to a nearby greenhouse where gnomes were tending seeds and

watering flowers.

"Hello!" she called.

The gnomes broke off from their work. "Hello, Trixi," said a gnome with 'Head Gardener' embroidered on his red hat. He smiled at the girls. "And you must be Ellie, Summer and Jasmine. My name is Percy. It's a pleasure to meet King Merry's special friends." He bowed deeply.

The other gnomes bowed, too.

"It's nice to meet you, Percy," said Jasmine, bowing back.

"The garden is beautiful," said Summer.

"Can we help you?" said Ellie.

"Well, that would be most kind," said Percy. "The tools are over here in the shed. You could do some weeding or watering, or perhaps you'd like to sing to the flowers – they really like that."

"I'd love to do that!" said Jasmine.

Just then, the sky started to darken. There was a loud clap of thunder. The girls and the Garden Gnomes looked round in alarm.

"What's happening?" said Percy. "It was sunny a moment ago."

Jasmine looked at the others. "Oh, no, you don't think that it's Queen Malice?"

"Don't worry," Percy said firmly, "she'll never get in to the Secret Garden, no one knows how, apart from us and King Merry…"

He trailed off as the gate swung open with a creak and Queen Malice strode through it. The gnomes grabbed rakes, hoes and spades, holding them as if they were weapons. The queen ignored them. She marched straight over to the girls, her pointy black boots trampling over the flowers. Dark, frizzy hair surrounded her pale face and her coal-black eyes glittered. "So, this is my brother's so-called *Secret* Garden, is it?" she sneered. "Well, it's not so secret anymore!"

"How did you get in?" demanded Jasmine.

"By telling the gate a secret, of course,"

said the queen, smirking. "My brother really should be more careful when he tells people how to open the door. I was listening behind the trees the whole time."

Summer gasped. So, it hadn't been an animal making the rustling noise – it had been Queen Malice!

"But why did you want to come in here?" said Ellie. Queen Malice hated pretty, happy places.

The queen cackled and raised her thunderstaff. "So, I can ruin the garden and stop the Petal Parade, of course!"

Queen Malice's Curse

"No, Queen Malice!" Trixi shouted bravely. "We won't let you ruin the garden or the parade. Go away!" She flew her leaf at the queen.

Queen Malice pointed her staff at the pixie and a thunderbolt shot out with a bang. Trixi swerved to avoid it.

CRASH! Trixi's leaf bumped into a tree and the little pixie tumbled to the ground.

"Trixi!" gasped Summer, running over

to check she was OK.

Trixi sat up, blinking, in a patch of thick, soft purple heather. She was shocked but luckily she wasn't hurt. She tapped her ring and her leaf flew straight back to her.

"Silly little pixie!" the queen hissed. "You should know better than to try and stop me. I'm going to place a curse on this garden."

She swept her thunderstaff around the garden.

"A secret I have told the gate,
And now the garden must face its fate.
Dry, dark and miserable it shall be,
And the Petal Parade is history!"

A flash of lightning exploded from the

top of the thunderstaff. The gnomes cried out as the light hit them and turned them into little statues, just like Nani's gnomes! Their brightly coloured clothes were now grey and their cheerful faces were shocked and fearful. Dark storm clouds covered the garden, blocking out the sun. More lightning crackled out of the thunderstaff as Queen

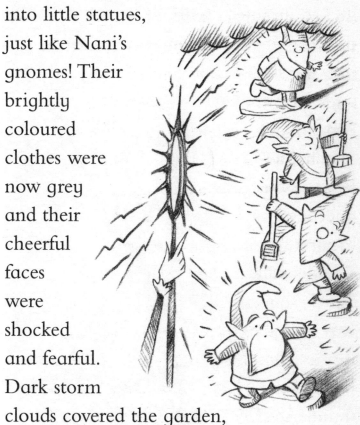

Malice pointed it at the fountain. All the water from the fountain's pool was sucked up into a swirling funnel and swept away into the sky.

Jasmine couldn't bear to watch. She leapt at the queen, trying to grab the thunderstaff, but the queen was too quick for her. She pointed the thunderstaff at the girls and Trixi and a

strong wind suddenly swept them all up into the air.

"Now, the garden is dark and miserable so all the flowers will die!" the queen cackled. "Don't bother trying to break the curse either, because the way to do it is a *secret*."

As she screeched the last word, Queen Malice vanished and the wind swept the girls and Trixi over the garden wall and dumped them on the ground outside the gate. Queen Malice's cackles faded as the wind died down.

"Oh no," Jasmine said, scrambling to her feet. The honeysuckle and roses that covered the walls had turned to spiky

thorn bushes with massive, prickly leaves covering their branches. "The poor garden. The poor gnomes."

"What are we going to do?" said Ellie.

"Queen Malice has ruined everything!" said Trixi, tears welling up in her eyes.

"We'll find a way to stop her," Summer promised. "Please don't cry, Trixi."

Jasmine nodded determinedly. "Let's get back into the garden for a start."

She ran to the gate and whispered her secret into the keyhole. But this time the gate didn't open. She rattled it but it stayed locked. "We can't get in!" she cried. "Queen Malice's spell must be stopping us."

"What's that sound?' said Ellie, going over to the gate and pressing her ear against it. She could hear faint singing.

*"Oh…come to the…Petal…Parade…
A day for…fun and…play…"*

The words had big gaps between them as if the singers were struggling to keep

going. "It's the songflowers," Ellie realised. "They don't sound well at all."

"Maybe we should go to the palace

and get King Merry," said Trixi.

"He's busy working on his float," said Jasmine. "Besides, remember what he said about happiness? The songflowers need it or they'll wilt!"

"But how do we get in?" Summer said.

"There must be a way," said Jasmine.

"How about your magic, Trixi?" said Ellie. "Could you use it to get us inside?"

"No," Trixi said, shaking her head sadly. "The Garden Gnomes put powerful spells on the gate. They thought that would keep Queen Malice out." She bit her lip. "They never thought she'd find out that she had to tell the gate a secret to get inside."

They all looked desperately at the walls and the beautiful locked gate.

"Maybe we could climb into the

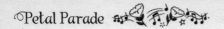

garden?" suggested Jasmine.

She went over to the wall and tried to climb up. "Ouch!" she cried, jumping back down again. It was impossible to

grip the sharp thorns. There was no way they would be able to climb the walls.

Jasmine rubbed her hand and frowned. There *had* to be a way to open the gate.

She thought back to what Queen Malice had said and an idea started to form in her head.

"Queen Malice said the way to break the curse is a secret," Jasmine said. "What if she meant *her* secret – the one she told to get into the Secret Garden?"

"It's worth a try," said Summer. "We'd just need to guess it."

"But how can we do that? Queen Malice's secret could be anything!" said Ellie in dismay.

"Let's all think about it," said Jasmine. "What would Queen Malice want to keep secret?"

They all thought hard. Summer's eyes widened suddenly. "I've got an idea!"

"Tell it to the gate!" Trixi said eagerly.

Summer went to the gate and whispered into the key hole. "Queen Malice's secret is that she likes cute, fluffy animals!"

The gate didn't open.

Summer looked disappointed.

"Let me try," said Ellie. She went to the gate. "Queen Malice is scared of thunder!"

Still, the gate stayed locked.

Jasmine had a go. "Queen Malice secretly likes the colour pink!"

Nothing happened.

Suddenly, there was a screeching, jeering sound from above. "Ha, ha, ha! You silly girls will never get in!"

They all looked up. Five dark shapes

with bat-like wings were circling high above them.

"It's Queen Malice's Storm Sprites!" Summer said in dismay.

Telling Secrets!

"Hee hee hee!" the Storm Sprites cackled gleefully as they flapped down towards the girls. They had long, bony fingers, leathery wings and mean little eyes. "Queen Malice has ruined the Petal Parade! There'll be no more flowers in the Secret Kingdom," one cried.

"Go away, you horrible things!" Ellie shouted crossly.

The sprites just cackled.

"Ignore them," Jasmine told the others. "Let's keep trying."

She went to the gate and lowered her voice so the sprites wouldn't hear what she was saying. "Queen Malice is scared of mice."

The gates didn't open.

The sprites shrieked and started diving at Jasmine, poking her with their fingers. She squealed and ran away from the gate.

The sprites flew to a nearby tree and sat in the branches, shouting out rude things.

"Weedy girls!"

"Slug brains!"

"You're all as slow as snails!"

"I wish they'd go away," said Ellie.

"It's impossible to think straight with them here!" said Summer.

"Unless...maybe they can help us," Jasmine said. "Maybe *they* know Queen Malice's secret."

"They'll never tell us even if they do," said Trixi.

A smile crept across Jasmine's face. "But what if we trick them into telling us?"

"How?" demanded Ellie.

Jasmine grinned. "Here, everyone huddle closer to me!"

The girls and Trixi squashed up together.

"Pretend that we're whispering," Jasmine hissed.

The others weren't sure what they were doing, but they trusted Jasmine, so they pretended to whisper.

The sprites stopped calling out insults.

"What are those girls doing?" one of the Storm Sprites said.

"I don't know," another sprite said.

"They're talking about something they don't want us to hear," said a third.

Jasmine looked over her shoulder and shouted, "Can you be quiet please? I'm trying to tell my best friends an important secret!"

"A secret!" The sprites' eyes gleamed as they came flapping over. "Ooh, we like secrets. Will you tell us?"

"No," Jasmine said. "I'm only telling Ellie, Summer and Trixi."

"But we want to know your secret!" whined one of the sprites.

Jasmine pulled the others in closer and lowered her voice to a faint whisper. "In a second, laugh really loudly and pretend I've just told you an amazing secret," she said. "OK, now!" She nudged them.

Ellie, Summer and Trixi all started to laugh loudly.

"Oh, that's brilliant, Jasmine!" said Summer. "It's so funny!"

"What a great secret!" exclaimed Ellie.

The sprites screeched in frustration. "Tell us! Tell us!"

"No," said Jasmine. "We're only telling

each other our secrets. Does anyone else know a secret?" she asked the others.

Trixi grinned and glanced at the sprites. "Oh, I do. It's a really good one about King Merry."

"A secret about King Merry!" gasped the first sprite.

"Oh, do tell us, Trixi!" said Summer.

"Tell us too!" begged another sprite. "Pleeeeeeeease."

"Well," Jasmine said, folding her arms and pretending to consider it. "I suppose they *could* listen, couldn't they, Trixi? But only if they told us a secret about Queen Malice in return."

"The sprites won't know a secret about Queen Malice," said Ellie.

"No, they're not clever enough," added Summer, trying not to giggle.

"We are!" shouted the first sprite. "We do know a secret about Queen Malice. A really good one!"

The girls winked at each other.

"All right then," said Jasmine. "It's got to be true though."

"Oh, it is!" the sprite cackled.

"Then it's a deal!" Jasmine said. "Trixi will tell you a secret about King Merry and you'll tell us a secret about Queen Malice."

All the sprites squealed in delight.

Summer felt her tummy flip in excitement. This was a brilliant plan. Now they might find out Queen Malice's secret and break the curse!

"Hang on... How do we know you won't trick us?" Ellie asked suddenly. "You might listen to King Merry's secret and not tell us yours."

Jasmine nodded. "Good point."

"I know," said Summer. "I'll count to three, then Trixi and the sprites can say their secrets at the same time."

Jasmine nodded.

Summer counted, "Three, two one…"

Trixi and the first sprite spoke together,

"Queen Malice is scared of the dark!"

"King Merry snores really loudly!"

The girls stared at each other, shocked. Was it possible? Could Queen Malice, who lived in gloomy Thunder Palace, really be afraid of the dark?

The sprites were falling about laughing. "King Merry snores! King Merry snores! Hee, hee, hee!"

"Will King Merry mind you telling them?" Summer whispered to Trixi worriedly.

The royal pixie shook her head. "He won't care at all, not if it saves the Secret Garden."

"Come on, let's see if it will!" said Jasmine, leaping to her feet and running to the gate. She crouched down and spoke into the keyhole. "Queen Malice's secret is that she's scared of the dark!"

There was a clap like a thunderbolt and the gate creaked open.

"It worked!" gasped Jasmine.

Ellie and Summer hugged each other and Trixi turned a loop-the-loop on her leaf. "Hooray!" she cried.

"You tricked us!" One of the Storm Sprites wailed. "You were telling secrets on purpose to get us to tell you Queen Malice's secret!"

"Yep!" Jasmine said with a grin.

The sprites screeched in fury.

Jasmine ignored them and hurried into the garden with Ellie and Summer close on her heels. The dark clouds overhead were clearing and golden sunshine was streaming into the garden. In all the flowerbeds, petals slowly unfurled as flowers greeted the sun. Even the daffodil-shaped fountain started to flow with water again. Shaking their heads and rubbing their eyes, the gnomes were coming back to life, their clothes brightly

coloured once again.

"Queen Malice's curse is broken!" Jasmine said in delight. Ellie whooped.

Thanks to the girls' happiness, the songflowers were able to pick up their drooping heads and raised them feebly towards the sunshine.

"They need water," said Summer. She looked around. "All the plants do."

"Gnomes, grab your watering cans!" cried Percy, the Head Gardener. "Quickly!"

The gnomes bustled over to the fountain. The pool the water flowed into was still empty, so they had to take turns filling up their watering cans from the fountain, catching the water drip by drip.

"It's going to take ages for them to fill up their watering cans," fretted Jasmine.

"And the songflowers don't look very

well at all," said Ellie. She looked up at the blue sky. "Oh, if only it would rain."

"At least the Petal Parade will go ahead!" said Trixi. "Once the songflowers have been watered they'll be ready to star in the parade!"

"Oh no, they won't!" shrieked a voice. The girls looked up and realised the Storm Sprites had flown through the

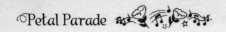

open gate. And worst of all, they each had a fat, grey misery drop in their hands. Ellie, Jasmine and Summer gasped. Misery drops were horrible! They made everything

they touched feel sad and unhappy.

"We'll water the plants," one of the sprites laughed.

"With our misery drops!" another cried.

And shrieking with laughter, the sprites started to throw their misery drops around the garden!

Misery Drop Magic

"No!" gasped Trixi. "The misery drops mustn't hit the songflowers or they'll never recover!"

As she spoke, a drop splashed onto a beautiful rose. Its glossy leaves instantly turned grey and its pink petals shrivelled. The girls watched in horror as, one by one, the petals drifted to the ground.

"Stop it!" shouted Jasmine, running over and trying to scare the Storm Sprites off by throwing clods of mud at them. Her heart was pounding. They couldn't let the sprites hurt King Merry's songflowers!

"Oh this is awful!" said Summer. "The flowers need water, but they need happiness – not misery!"

"Summer, you've just given me a perfect idea!" Trixi exclaimed.

She flew up high and tapped her magic pixie ring.

"Turn the drops from miserable to bright
Bring the garden happiness and light!"

There was a bright flash of light and suddenly the grey misery drops turned clear and sparkling. The sprites yelled in surprise and dropped them. As the shimmering drops fell on the flowers, the plants sprang up, happy and healthy. The gnomes put down their watering cans and cheered.

"NO!" the Storm Sprites shrieked in dismay.

"Ugh! They're not misery drops, they're happy drops!" one sprite said, throwing his drop on the ground in disgust. The flower it splashed looked bigger and more beautiful than before.

"Thanks for watering the garden for us!" Ellie called cheekily.

All around them, the garden sprang to life again, the magic drops of happiness making the flowers healthier and stronger than ever before.

Jasmine, Summer and Ellie swung each other round by the hands and their happiness made the songflowers grow even taller. They opened and shut their petals and started to sing.

"Oh come to the Petal Parade,
A day for fun and play.
Oh come to the Petal Parade,
Hip, hip, hip...hooray!"

Jasmine, Summer and Ellie joined in with the song. The gnomes started to sing along too, using their watering cans as drums. The garden was full of joy and the plants grew before the girls' eyes. Fragrant roses and sweet peas climbed up the walls, pretty pansies and marigolds spilled out of pots, and lilies that

reminded Jasmine of trumpets opened their petals in bursts of pink and white.

"STOP!"

They all swung round. Queen Malice was at the gate. She was glaring furiously at the garden.

"You fools! You good-for-nothing flapping creatures! You've ruined everything!" she shrieked at the Storm Sprites. "Get back to Thunder

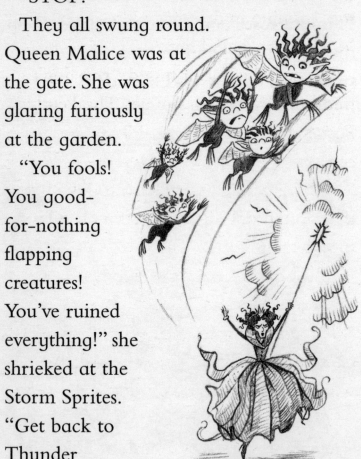

Castle right away!"

The Storm Sprites hastily flew off.

"Your spell is broken, Queen Malice!" said Jasmine in delight. "Now, go away. You're not wanted here."

"I'll go," the queen hissed. "But don't think you've beaten me yet. The Petal Parade won't take place. I'll make sure of that!"

She banged her thunderstaff down on the ground and disappeared with a loud thunderclap.

"She's gone!" cried the gnomes. "Hooray! Hooray!"

The girls hugged each other. "I don't care what she says," Jasmine said. "We won't let her spoil the parade."

"Never!" declared Ellie.

Just then there was a flash of light and

a rainbow appeared in the sky.

"Look! The rainbow slide!" cried Summer, pointing. The rainbow slide led from the pond outside the Enchanted Palace to anywhere in the Secret Kingdom. A moment later, King Merry came whizzing down it.

"King Merry!" exclaimed

Trixi delightedly as the king somersaulted over and landed on his bottom on a soft pile of grass.

"Goodness, gracious me," he said as the girls ran over to help him up. "The garden's looking wonderful, my dears."

Jasmine, Ellie and Summer looked at each other, their eyes wide.

"It wasn't a minute ago!" said Ellie.

The girls explained everything that had happened.

King Merry was so shocked he had to sit down again on a stone bench. "Oh that sister of mine. What will she think of next?" He shook his head. "It sounds like you were very clever to guess her secret. I can't believe she's still scared of the dark after all these years." He chuckled. "When we were little she never could fall asleep without a night-light!"

"Do you mind me telling the sprites your secret, King Merry?" Trixi asked.

"Not at all! I expect anyone who lives near the palace has heard my snoring." King Merry took a breath. "Well, it sounds like you've been having a very adventurous time. I think we need a nice picnic to recover. What do you say?"

"Oh, yes please!" the girls said.

Trixi conjured up an amazing picnic. There were soft blankets and purple cushions to sit on, plates of lavender shortbread, little cakes decorated with sugared violets, and pitchers full of rose lemonade. All the gnomes joined in as the plants nodded their heads in the sunshine.

"This is the best picnic ever," Ellie said happily, as she lay back in the sun,

feeling very full of biscuits and cake.

"It has been splendid, but now it's time for you to go home, I think," said King Merry. "I'll send a message tomorrow and you can come back for the Petal Parade. After all, it's only going ahead because of you."

The girls stood up and held hands.

"We'll see you tomorrow, King Merry," said Summer.

Trixi flew over on her leaf and kissed each of the girls on the nose. Then she tapped her ring. Sparkles flew out and surrounded the girls.

"Goodbye!" called the gnomes, King Merry and Trixi.

The girls spun away and landed safely back in Jasmine's bedroom.

"Wow," said Jasmine, her eyes shining. "That was an incredible adventure."

"I love the Secret Garden," said Summer, sighing happily.

"Me too. We'll have to be on the lookout for Queen Malice tomorrow," said Ellie. "I bet she'll try and do something horrible."

"Well, we'll be ready for her!" said Jasmine firmly.

"Girls!" Jasmine's grandma called to them. Luckily no time ever passed while the girls were away in the Secret Kingdom, so Nani hadn't realised they'd been gone. After tucking the Magic Box safely into Ellie's backpack, they went outside. Nani was setting out lunch on the garden table. There were warm samosas and little chicken sandwiches.

"I didn't think I could eat a single thing more when we left the Secret Kingdom," Jasmine whispered to the others as she breathed in the spicy smell of the samosas. "But maybe I can."

"Come and sit down," called Nani.

They joined her at the table and started filling their plates.

"This looks delicious," Summer said to Nani. "Thank you."

Nani smiled. "Gardening always works up an appetite, that's what I say."

"So does stopping Queen Malice," Jasmine whispered to the others as her grandma went back into the house to fetch some drinks.

They grinned at each other. If only Nani knew what they had been doing!

Ellie picked up a sandwich. "This will

give us lots of energy. We'll probably need it tomorrow."

"Whatever happens we'll be ready," said Jasmine.

"We'll make sure the Petal Parade is a success," said Summer.

The friends all grinned. They couldn't wait for their next adventure to start!

Book Two

Contents

Lucky Ladybird

"Oh, come to the Petal Parade," Jasmine sang as she watered a pot of marigolds in her garden with Summer and Ellie. *"A day for fun and play…"*

Summer grinned as she put down her watering can. "Hopefully, we *will* be going to the Petal Parade very soon," she whispered. It was the day after their last visit to the Secret Kingdom, and she couldn't wait to go back! All three girls had dressed in flower-patterned outfits especially!

A ladybird landed on Summer's hand, the black spots standing out on its shiny red back. Summer lifted her hand close to her face so she could study the insect.

With its little antennae and black face, it was very cute.

"Did you know that it's lucky to have a ladybird land on you?" said

Nani, coming out of the house with a gardening magazine and a pen. "You should make a wish before it flies away."

Summer didn't hesitate. *I wish that the Petal Parade is a big success,* she thought quickly, remembering Queen Malice's threats from the day before.

The little ladybird flew away from Summer's hand. "Ladybirds are my favourite type of insect," Nani said, sitting down on a sun lounger. "They're a gardener's best friend. They eat all the nasty pests that feast on plants." Nani opened her gardening magazine. "Now, let me see if I can finish this crossword. Maybe you girls can help me? I've got a clue here: *tall yellow flower.* The answer is nine letters long and starts with an 'S'."

"Sunflower!" Jasmine, Ellie and Summer

all cried at the same time.

Nani smiled. "I think you're right, girls. Thank you very much." She wrote down the answer. "Now, the next question is: *What helps plants grow strong?*"

"Happiness!" Jasmine said immediately.

Nani chuckled. "Oh, Jasmine, you and your imagination! Plants don't need happiness, but they *do* need light and water. Yes, I think *light* is the answer I'm looking for." She filled in the letters.

Jasmine, Ellie and Summer exchanged looks. Maybe plants in their world didn't need happiness to grow, but in the Secret Kingdom they certainly did!

Nani yawned. "All this sunshine is making me sleepy. I think I'll just shut my eyes for a few minutes."

She put her magazine down and a few minutes later she was snoring softly.

"She's just like King Merry!" Jasmine whispered with a grin. The Secret Kingdom's ruler snored, too.

"Should we go and check the Magic Box?" Ellie said. "Trixi might have sent us a message by now."

Summer and Jasmine nodded eagerly. Ellie picked up her bag and they hurried behind a tree at the bottom of the garden. As she opened her bag, they all caught their breath in excitement. Sparkling light was shining out of it!

"There *is* a message!" breathed Summer happily.

Jasmine peeked round the tree. Her grandmother was still dozing in the sun. Ellie pulled the box out and they read the words swirling across its mirrored lid.

"The floats are done,
Flowers dance in the sun,
Please come to the garden
To have some fun!"

"We don't need the map to solve the riddle today," said Jasmine. "We know exactly where we're going!"

They all put their hands on the gems on the box's lid. "The Secret Garden!" they called together.

With a flash of bright light, the box opened and Trixi came zooming out on her leaf. She was wearing a short white skirt, white boots and a white jacket with golden buttons. She was twirling a silver baton in her hand. "Hello, girls!" she called as she skidded her flying leaf to a halt.

"Hi, Trixi. Is it time for the Petal Parade?" Ellie asked.

Trixi threw her baton into the air and caught it. "It certainly is!"

"Has there been any sign of Queen Malice?" Summer asked anxiously.

"No," said Trixi happily. "Hopefully she'll stay far away from the parade."

Summer didn't think that was very likely, but the little pixie looked so excited she didn't have the heart to say so.

Trixi grinned. "What are we waiting for? Hold hands, it's time to go!"

King Merry's Fabulous Float

Trixi tapped her ring and whisked the girls away in a golden cloud. They landed just outside the Secret Garden. As the sparkles cleared, Summer looked down at their clothes. Would they be wearing gardening smocks and wellies again? But this time Trixi hadn't changed their flowery outfits. Instead, she'd magically put sparkles on each flower so that they glittered as much as the special tiaras that had appeared on their heads.

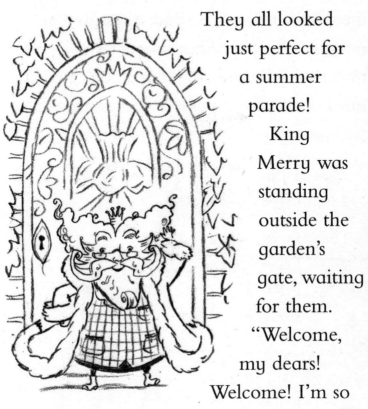

They all looked just perfect for a summer parade!

King Merry was standing outside the garden's gate, waiting for them.

"Welcome, my dears! Welcome! I'm so glad you're here. I can't wait to show you my float. The Garden Gnomes have been hard at work making it ever since you left yesterday. Do come and see it."

He went to the gate and whispered

into the keyhole. The gate swung open and the girls gasped as they saw a beautiful float on the other side. It looked just like the Enchanted Palace, only it was completely made out of flowers!

There were pink turrets made out of carnations, with red roses dotting the walls just as rubies studded the walls of the real palace. Bright yellow songflowers were planted all around the base of the float. Gnomes were hurrying around it adding flowers here and there.

"Incredible!" Ellie breathed.

Summer and Jasmine just nodded in amazement. The float was so beautiful!

King Merry beamed. "Haven't the gnomes done a wonderful job? Watch this." He clapped his hands and the songflowers started to sing:

"Oh, come to the Petal Parade,
A day for fun and play.
Oh come to the Petal Parade,
Hip, hip, hip...hooray!"

The girls cheered in delight and Trixi turned a loop-the-loop in the air.

King Merry scratched his head. "The float looks lovely, but I feel like I've forgotten something. What could it be..."

Grinning, Trixi tapped her pixie ring and the float magically lifted into the air. It hovered over the grass for a moment then came floating out of the garden, coming to rest beside them.

"Wow!" exclaimed Jasmine. "A float that really floats!"

"Thank you, Trixi," chuckled King Merry. "Oh, I do hope my float makes people happy. We need their happiness to make the magic breeze that scatters petals and seeds around the kingdom."

"I'm sure your float will make everyone who sees it *very* happy!" said Summer.

King Merry smiled in relief. "The other floats should be here very soon. They're coming from all corners of the Secret Kingdom. All the floats will meet here and then parade to the palace." He looked down at his gardening waistcoat and wellies. "I should get back to the palace to get changed..."

He was interrupted by a rumble of thunder. "Oh, dearie me. I hope there isn't going to be a rain storm."

The girls looked at each other in alarm.

Jasmine turned anxiously to the king. "King Merry, do you think that—"

CRASH! There was a strong gust of wind, then a rumble of thunder and a bright fork of lightning tore through the sky. They all blinked. Opening their eyes, they saw Queen Malice standing beside the beautiful float. Her black eyes glittered in her pale face. "So, this is your precious float, brother," she hissed. "This is what you think will make everyone at the parade *happy*?" She spat the word out nastily.

King Merry pushed his spectacles firmly up his nose. "Yes, it is. And you're not going to spoil things, sister. Go back to Thunder Castle." A mischievous, twinkle lit up his eyes. "Unless you're too scared of the dark there, of course."

Jasmine, Ellie and Summer couldn't help themselves. Despite their worry at seeing the horrid queen, they all giggled.

"Oh, so you think I'm funny, do you?" Queen Malice shrieked in fury.

"Well, let's see how funny you think this is!" She turned and pointed her thunderstaff at the float and chanted:

"Flowers to
thorns,
Leaves to
weeds,
Snap traps appear,
Ready to feed!"

A thunderbolt flew out of the end

of her staff and hit the beautiful palace float. It instantly transformed into a mountain of weeds and thorny plants.

The songflowers had vanished. Now, ugly plants with big green heads instead of flowers stood in their place. When they opened their mouths, they looked even more horrid – each plant had rows of sharp white teeth!

"No!" gasped the girls.

"Sister!" thundered the king.

Queen Malice screeched. "Now, see how much happiness your precious float brings, brother. I told you I would ruin the parade. You should have believed me!" She banged her thunderstaff down on the ground and disappeared in a puff of black smoke.

Jasmine, Summer and Ellie looked at the float in dismay – it was completely ruined!

Ruined!

Tears welled up in King Merry's eyes. Summer ran to comfort him. "Oh, King Merry. Don't worry. It'll be all right," she said, hugging him.

"But how?" he sniffled as Trixi magicked up a big red-and-white spotty hanky for him. He blew his nose nosily.

"My lovely float is ruined. Now people won't be happy and the Petal Parade's magic won't work."

"There are still all the other floats," said Jasmine, remembering what the king had said about all the other floats arriving soon. "I'm sure they'll make everyone happy enough for the magic to work."

"And maybe we can help the gnomes fix your float," said Ellie. "We can use some more flowers and make it look good again."

Summer nodded. "Why don't you go back to the palace and get ready, King Merry? We'll sort things out here."

"Summer's right," said Trixi. "We'll soon repair the float if we all work together."

King Merry took a deep breath. "You're right. Thank you, my dear friends. I don't know what I would do without you. The parade shall go on! Trixi, please send me back to the palace."

"Of course, Your Majesty," Trixi said. She tapped her pixie ring. A cloud of sparkles surrounded King Merry and he vanished.

Jasmine straightened her shoulders.

"Right, time for action," she said, looking at the ruined float. "What we need to do is to get rid of all those nasty weeds, then we'll go into the garden and find some more flowers."

"Let's pull the snap traps up first," Ellie said. She went over to the float and grabbed one of the ugly plants by the stalk.

SNAP!

"Hey!" Ellie yelled. She jumped back as the plant snapped at her with its sharp teeth.

Another plant reared up and lunged at Trixi, nearly catching her leaf in its teeth.

"Yikes!" cried Trixi, flying out of the way just in time. "That was close!"

"Not close enough, pixie!" the snap trap said in a horrible scratchy voice. Its leaves flapped as it stretched its jaws up towards her, snapping again and again.

"The snap traps can talk!" Summer gasped in amazement.

"Of course we can!" snapped another plant crossly.

"Stay away from us," one said, baring its teeth. "Or we'll bite your ankles."

"And munch your fingers and nibble your ears!" said another, laughing so hard its leaves shook.

"Help!" Trixi squealed as the plant that had been stretching towards her suddenly started flapping its leaves like wings. Then, with a big tug, it pulled itself free of the soil and flapped into the air!

The girls yelled in surprise as all the other snap traps followed it.

"They're not just snap traps – they're FLYING snap traps!" cried Ellie.

The horrible plants started to chase Trixi around, their mouths opening and shutting as they flew.

"Get that pixie's leaf!" one shouted. "Chomp it up!"

"Oh no!" gasped Trixi, zig-zagging frantically through the air.

"Stop it! Stop it!" shouted Jasmine.

But the snap traps took no notice. "Snap! Snap! Tasty leaf!" they chanted as

they charged after Trixi.

The gnomes chased the snap traps with their rakes and spades, trying to knock them out of the sky.

Trixi dodged them, swooping through the air. "Come here, Trixi!" Jasmine

called. "We'll protect you!"

The pixie flew down gratefully and landed on Jasmine's shoulder. Summer and Ellie stood back to back with Jasmine, keeping the horrible plants away.

"Leave Trixi alone!" shouted Summer.

The snap traps formed a circle round the girls. "Snap! Snap! We're going to gobble her leaf!" one laughed.

"No you're not!" cried Ellie. "Look over there!" She pointed through the trees.

"The other floats!" exclaimed Summer, her heart lifting as she saw a procession of colourful floats drifting towards them in the sky. A band of brownies playing musical instruments were marching ahead of them, leading all the floats to the Secret Garden.

"Hooray!" cheered Jasmine.

The floats were all different shapes and sizes but they were all covered in flowers, filling the air with sweet scents. The first, from Fairytale Forest, had a carpet of woodland flowers and trees with books growing on the branches.

"Look! It's the book brownies!" cried Summer, waving to the brownies riding on the float.

Next came a float from Serenity Island piled high with exotic blossoms. The islanders on it all were wearing garlands of orchids and dancing to soothing music.

Jasmine remembered the dance they'd learned on Serenity Island and swayed along with the dancers.

The islanders' float was followed by one from Lily Pad Lake with a rock pool dotted with giant water lilies. Two water nymphs with pale blue skin and silver hair were playing in the water. The girls giggled as drops of water splashed them.

A float covered with wild meadow flowers and big baskets of juicy apples came next. Six unicorns with flowers braided into their manes and tails pranced proudly on it.

"Littlehorn! Hello!" called Ellie to their unicorn friend. Littlehorn lowered her horn in greeting.

"See, you can't stop the parade!" Jasmine told the snap traps triumphantly.

But the snap traps had stopped looking at Trixi's leaf and were staring at the flowery floats hungrily.

"Oh no!" Summer cried as the snap traps turned. "They're going to eat the flower floats!"

Spotty Bugs to the Rescue!

The snap traps flew straight towards the floats, their jaws chomping and their leaves flapping hard.

"No!" gasped Summer as Queen Malice's nasty plants swarmed around the floats. "Look what they're doing!"

Bits of leaves and petals flew up into the sky like confetti as the snap traps tore into the floats. Their sharp teeth munched and crunched as they pulled the floats apart with their sharp teeth.

CRACK! The snap traps ripped branches off the brownies' trees.

SPLAT! They munched the giant lily pads in the water nymphs' pond.

YANK! Queen Malice's nasty plants snatched the orchid garlands off the islanders' necks.

The unicorns charged at the snap traps, but the flying plants just dodged away and started gobbling up the colourful flowers that covered their float.

"This is awful!" cried Ellie above the noise. "We've got to stop them."

The girls all thought desperately, trying to come up with a plan.

"How can we get rid of those horrible pests?" wondered Jasmine in despair.

The word 'pests' gave Summer a thought... "Hang on," she said to the others. "Nani said that ladybirds eat garden pests. Does the Secret Kingdom have ladybirds, too?"

She ran to Percy, the head gardener,

who was trying to swat a snap trap with his rake. "Percy, in the Other Realm we have bugs called ladybirds that eat garden pests. Do you have anything like that here?"

"Spotty bugs," Percy replied immediately. "They keep all kinds of pests out of the Secret Garden. But they don't eat plants."

"Hmmm, I wonder if the snap traps will know that?" Jasmine said thoughtfully.

"Do you think they could scare the snap traps away?" Summer asked.

"Of course! What a clever idea," Percy said. "Leave it to me!"

He whistled loudly. The other gnomes heard him and started to join in. Soon the air was full of the sound

of whistling and whirring. Hundreds of creatures came flying out over the walls of the Secret Garden, their wings beating so quickly they were a blur!

"They look like giant ladybirds," gasped Jasmine.

"But more colourful!" said Summer in awe. Their shiny backs were covered in big spots in every colour of the rainbow!

Percy gathered the spotty bugs around him. "Friends," he began solemnly, "some pests have been harming our flowers." Lowering his voice to a whisper, he added, "can you scare the snap traps away

by pretending that you want to eat them?"

The spotty bugs all nodded their heads eagerly.

"My spotty bug friends are hungry for their lunch," Percy shouted. "So make it *snappy*!"

The spotty bugs flew straight at the snap traps, their wings whirring. Screeching in alarm, the snap traps started flying away from the floats.

"Yum!" one of the spotty bugs called as it got closer. "Snap traps, my favourite!"

"Help!" The snap traps' leaves flapped wildly as they tried to escape from the big bugs. The plants bumped into each other, wailing and shrieking, as the spotty bugs chased them in circles.

"Good work, spotty bugs!" Ellie called, trying not to giggle. "Eat them all up!"

"Let's get out of here!" The snap traps flapped their leaves as fast as they could and flew away in the direction of Thunder Castle. The spotty bugs chased after them until the snap traps were just tiny dots on the horizon.

"They've gone!" said Jasmine, happily.

"That was a brilliant idea," said Ellie.

"But look at the mess they've made!" said Summer in dismay. The flowers that had covered the beautiful floats were scattered all over the ground. Ragged holes gaped in the displays. The gnomes were helping the islanders gather up the orchid petals while the water nymphs tried to mend their lily pads. The book brownies were picking up books and smoothing their crumpled pages, while the unicorns used their horns to try and

nudge the remaining flowers on their float back into place.

Just then the spotty bugs came flying back. They landed by the garden gate.

"Thank you very much, my friends," Percy said. "Now why don't we fetch you something you really *do* like to eat?"

The spotty bugs nodded their heads and flapped their wings in reply. The gnomes hurried into the garden and returned with two wheelbarrows filled with glittering golden liquid.

"What's that?" Ellie asked.

"Honeysuckle nectar," Percy told her. "We grow honeysuckle in the garden and collect the nectar from its flowers. The spotty bugs love it."

The gnomes handed out bell-shaped flowers full of nectar, which the spotty bugs slurped happily.

Then one of the gnomes gave each of the girls a flower cup filled with honeysuckle nectar – there was even a tiny one for Trixi!

"Try some," urged Percy. "I'm sure you'll like it."

"Mmm," said Jasmine, taking a sip. The liquid tasted as if it was made of honey and sunshine. It was wonderfully light and sweet. "Oh, wow! I can see why the spotty bugs love it so much."

"Yum!" Ellie agreed. "It's delicious!"

Summer finished her honeysuckle nectar and licked her lips. "Let's start helping with the floats," she said, heading toward the garden gate. "We just need to get some more flowers from the garden and...oh!"

She stopped in surprise. Ellie and Jasmine joined her.

"What's the matter?" Jasmine started to say but then she saw what Summer was staring at. Yesterday, the Secret Garden had been overflowing with flowers of every colour. Now, the flowerbeds were bare and empty – there were no flowers anywhere!

The Parade Must Go On

"What's happened to the garden, Percy?" said Ellie in astonishment.

"We used all the flowers up to make King Merry's float," the old gnome said sadly. "We've planted new ones but they won't bloom until next spring."

Ellie's heart sank. "If there are no flowers then we can't repair the floats."

"Or build a new one for King Merry," said Jasmine.

"What are we going to do?" said Summer. "If there aren't any floats no one will be happy and the Petal Parade's magic won't work!"

The girls exchanged worried looks.

"Trixi," Jasmine asked. "Could you magic up some more flowers?"

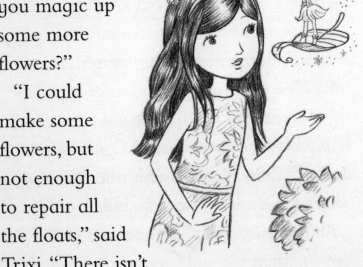

"I could make some flowers, but not enough to repair all the floats," said Trixi. "There isn't enough time." She rubbed her forehead. "Oh, this is impossible."

Ellie thought quickly. "What about getting flowers from somewhere else? The Secret Kingdom has lots of flowers everywhere – not just here in the garden."

"Good idea!" said Jasmine. "There's Fairytale Forest and Wildflower Wood."

"Dream Dale," added Summer. "And the mountains near Jewel Cavern."

"But how can we collect enough flowers before the parade starts?" asked Trixi. "We don't have time to go to all those different places."

"What about the spotty bugs?" Ellie said suddenly. She turned to Percy. "Would the spotty bugs be able to fly around the kingdom to collect more flowers for us?"

"I'm sure they would," said Percy. "What do you think, my friends?" he asked the spotty bugs. "Will you help?"

The spotty bugs cheerfully nodded.

"Oh, please hurry," Summer pleaded. "Bring back all the flowers you can."

The gnomes ran to fetch baskets, giving one to each of the spotty bugs. With a whirring of wings, the bugs set off in all different directions, holding their baskets with their legs.

Everyone waved goodbye.

"Come back soon!" Percy called.

Jasmine looked around at the ruined floats. The gnomes, brownies, unicorns and nymphs were still trying to patch them up as best they could. She gripped her friends' hands in hers. "In the meantime, we've got work to do here!"

The girls each ran to help with a different float. Ellie went over to the Lily Pad Lake float. The nymphs were trying to arrange the remaining water lilies as

prettily as they could on the surface of the glittering water.

Ellie picked up a big lily that was lying on the ground. Luckily, it wasn't damaged. "Here, this one is OK," she said, handing it to the nymphs. "And this one." She gave them another flower.

"Thank you!" said the nymphs. "Do you want to come and join us?"

"Yes, please," Ellie said, climbing on to the float.

One of the nymphs smiled shyly at her. "Hi, I'm Thalia. My cousin Nadia said to say hello if I saw you. She stayed at home to look after Curly."

Ellie smiled. Nadia was a water nymph they had made friends with when they had visited Clearsplash Waterfall. Curly was her giant pet water snail.

"Is this your first Petal Parade?" Ellie asked, as she helped the nymphs repair the float.

Thalia nodded. "I'm so excited."

"Me too!" said Ellie.

Meanwhile, Summer was helping the six unicorns use the flowers that had been woven into their manes and tails to start to patch up the holes in their float.

One of them was her friend, Littlehorn, who she'd met one of the very first times the girls had come to the Secret Kingdom.

As they worked on the float, Littlehorn told Summer that her mother, Silvertail, the

leader of the unicorn, was waiting at the palace to greet the floats. "It's the first year she's let me lead the float on my own," said Littlehorn, swishing her tail.

"She's going to be so disappointed when she sees what's happened to it."

"Don't feel bad. You couldn't have stopped the snap traps," Summer said, giving the young unicorn a hug. "We'll do everything we can to make the floats look good for the parade." She glanced anxiously at the sky. She hoped the spotty bugs would come back soon. Time was ticking by and it was nearly time for the parade to begin.

Jasmine was watching the sky too as she helped the book brownies repair their float. "Trixi, how long is it until the parade starts?" she called, tucking a flower back into place.

"Not long now," said Trixi, tapping her ring and conjuring up a big bouquet of woodland daisies to fill a hole in the brownies' float. "Oh dear, I don't think we're going to be ready in time."

"We might be! Look!" said Jasmine, pointing at the horizon. "Here come the spotty bugs!"

The spotty bugs were flying back towards them from all different directions. Their baskets were overflowing with beautiful, brightly coloured blooms.

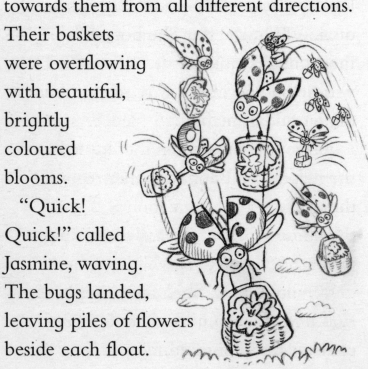

"Quick! Quick!" called Jasmine, waving. The bugs landed, leaving piles of flowers beside each float.

Everyone cheered and started rushing round to fix the floats.

Ellie, Summer and Jasmine went over to King Merry's ruined float. All the flowers had gone, leaving it completely bare.

"What should we do? King Merry must have a float," said Ellie. The girls looked at it in dismay. How could they make it into something fit for the jolly little king?

"Maybe we could try making a smaller model of the Enchanted Palace," said Ellie, picking up some red poppies. "Or perhaps we could make a crown or a throne?"

"We haven't got enough time," said Jasmine. "King Merry will be arriving any minute now." She racked her brains. What could they make quickly? She couldn't think of anything.

"There must be *something* we can do," Summer said desperately.

"Maybe we can just scatter some flowers on top of the float." Jasmine suggested. She looked at the pretty blossoms the gnomes were piling up. "It would be better than nothing."

"Oh no! We're too late," Ellie said,

pointing to the sky. "Look!"

Summer and Jasmine gazed up at where she was pointing. An enormous rainbow was beginning to appear in the sky. "It's King Merry's rainbow slide," said Summer. "King Merry is on his way!"

A Rainbow Float

An idea popped into Jasmine's head. "That's it!" she gasped. "Of course! The rainbow slide!" She looked at the flowers. "We could make it out of all these flowers. It would be perfect for King Merry's float and it won't take long to make at all. Trixi, can you get rid of the palace shape?"

"Of course!" Trixi tapped her pixie ring and suddenly the float was empy.

"Brilliant," Jasmine said. "Now quick! Let's make a rainbow!"

Everyone grabbed handfuls of flowers and started to build a rainbow. The gnomes and their friends from the other floats raced over to help before the little king arrived. First, the Garden Gnomes bent long sticks of cane into the shape of an arc. Everyone decorated it with a layer of red poppies from Mystic Meadow. Then they added orangey-pink cherry blossom

from Dream Dale and yellow daffodils from Wildflower Wood.

"Thanks for your help, Littlehorn," Summer said as the unicorn nudged some bright orange marigolds into place.

"These will be perfect for the blue layer," cried Ellie, holding up a big bunch of sweet-smelling bluebells.

As everyone added more and more flowers to the coloured layers, the rainbow started to take shape. Trixi flew around, adding a layer of glossy green leaves. The girls and their helpers had just finished adding the final layers of deep blue pansies, and purple violets when there was the sound of a cheerful voice. "Wheeeeee!"

King Merry came whooshing down the real rainbow slide, landing in the remaining pile of flowers with a soft thump. Cherry blossoms flew up into the air, some pink petals catching in his white curly hair. The girls ran over to help King Merry as he struggled to his feet. He had changed out of his gardening clothes and was now wearing

a smart white-and-gold suit with a rainbow-coloured cloak embroidered with gold flowers.

"Crowns and sceptres!" he exclaimed, pointing at the new float. "Where did this beautiful rainbow float come from?"

"We made it for you, Your Majesty," said Jasmine. "Everyone helped."

"We didn't want you to miss out on having a float in the procession," Ellie explained.

"And we wanted to make sure everyone who comes to the parade feels really happy," Summer added.

King Merry blushed bright red and clasped his hands together. "Well, it has certainly made *me* very happy. It even matches my cloak. Thank you!" he cried to everyone. They all cheered.

"We should start the parade, Your Majesty," said Trixi. "Everyone will be gathering in the villages, waiting for the floats to pass by."

"Hop on to your floats, everyone!" cried the little king. He looked at Trixi. "Trixi, maybe you can assist with some chairs for me and my friends on my new float..."

Trixi grinned. "Of course, Your Majesty!"

She tapped her ring and a golden throne appeared on the float along with three comfy chairs covered with rainbow-striped cushions for the girls.

The girls climbed on to the float and helped King Merry on board. They all sat down and then the Garden Gnomes brought them baskets of fragrant petals and seeds to throw into the air.

Trixi took her place at the very front of the parade, twirling her baton as she got ready to lead the brownie band.

King Merry shook his head. "I love this new float but it's such a shame we don't have the songflowers to sing as we parade. It would have made the crowds so very happy. We need lots of happiness to make enough magic to scatter the petals and seeds right across the whole of the kingdom."

"We can sing instead!" Jasmine suggested. "We know the words to the songflowers' parade song."

"Will you teach us it?" called Thalia, the water nymph.

"Of course!" said Jasmine. She stood up

on the Rainbow Float and sang the song, conducting the others with her hands.

"Oh, come to the Petal Parade,
A day for fun and play.
Oh come to the Petal Parade,
Hip, hip, hip…hooray!"

Ellie and Summer joined in and soon everyone else did too. Their voices rose, lifting up to the blue sky.

King Merry beamed. "Let the Petal Parade begin!" he cried.

King Merry's float rose into the air and followed the marching band through the woods. As the floats came out of the trees, the girls saw there were elves, brownies and pixies lining the path, waving banners and cheering.

King Merry and the girls took out handfuls of petals and seeds and threw them into the air. They spiralled upwards and disappeared, blown by the magic breeze, with a few falling on to the pretty village. Wherever they landed, beautiful

new flowers appeared.

The girls sang as they threw the petals into the air. Summer looked behind and saw that everyone on the other floats were throwing handfuls of petals and seeds too. As the villagers joined in with the song, the air was filled with swirling clouds of sweet-smelling petals.

"The Petal Parade is going to be a success after all!" cried Ellie in delight.

"Listen to all the singing! Everyone is so happy – this is going to be the best parade ever!" said King Merry.

"I don't think so!" snapped a horribly familiar voice. The sky turned dark as storm clouds blotted out the sun.

"Queen Malice!" everyone cried as the horrid queen came swooping down from the sky.

The Petal Parade

"Yes, it's me!" hissed the queen, standing on a small black storm cloud. She pulled a face. "Those flowers smell hideous! And your singing is dreadful! This happiness must stop!" She raised her thunderstaff and the cloud floated higher and grew bigger. "I shall make it rain and rain until all the flowers are soggy and spoiled. Prepare to get very, VERY wet!"

The crowd gasped, but Jasmine jumped to her feet. "Wait a moment, Queen Malice. If you do that, then we'll tell everyone your secret."

Queen Malice hesitated, her thunderstaff still raised. "You wouldn't."

"Oh, we would!" cried Ellie.

"Yes," said Summer quickly. "If you don't go away right now, we'll tell everyone that you're afraid of the—"

"Nooooo!" screamed the nasty queen. With a shriek of rage, she banged her thunderstaff and vanished in a flash of lightning.

Summer, Ellie and Jasmine looked at each other and started to giggle. "Well, that stopped her," said Jasmine.

"Oh, my sister," said King Merry, shaking his head. "Why does she always try and spoil things?"

Because she's Queen Malice," said Ellie. "But at least she didn't succeed this time."

"King Merry," Trixi called as she sped over on her leaf. "Everyone's stopped singing."

The girls looked round. The villagers had dropped their banners and were huddling together, chattering nervously and pointing to where Queen Malice had been. The petals that had been whirling magically in the air started dropping like autumn leaves.

"Oh no," said Summer. "Nobody's happy, so the magic breeze has stopped blowing."

"Quick, we'd better cheer everyone up!" cried Jasmine. "Brownies, please play your music as loudly as you can!"

The brownie band started playing their instruments again and the girls began to sing the songflowers' song.

"Come on, everyone, join in!" Jasmine urged the crowd. "*Oh come to the Petal Parade, a day for fun and play…*"

One by one, the villagers started to sing the song. Their voices rose and grew louder and happier as more people joined in. The petals whirled back into the air and flew away across the Secret Kingdom.

"The magic's working again!" King Merry exclaimed in delight. "Oh, thank you! Thank you!"

The girls sang all the way to the Enchanted Palace. There were even more people and magical creatures waiting by the golden gates, including Silvertail who trotted over and nuzzled Littlehorn proudly. As the crowds cheered and whooped, the elf butlers threw open the palace gates and everyone climbed off the floats. A huge feast had been laid out in the garden. Tables were piled high with tiny sandwiches in the shape of flowers, bowls of the sweetest dewberries and sugar plums, and jugs of ice-cold fruit punch. There were banks of soft cherry blossom to sit on and the scent of roses and honeysuckle filled the air.

The brownie band played happily and

soon everyone was dancing and eating and having fun.

"This is the best garden party I've ever been to," Ellie said contentedly.

"Just think," said Summer. "All around the Secret Kingdom, petals and seeds are landing and new flowers will be springing up to make people happy all year long."

"There's one growing already," said Jasmine, pointing to a seedling nudging its way out of the soil. Going over to take a closer look, the girls heard the faint sound of a voice coming from its yellow bud. "*Oh come to the petal parade…*"

A songflower! "King Merry!" the girls called excitedly.

King Merry hurried over to them with Trixi flying beside him.

"Look! Some new songflowers are growing!" Jasmine said. "Some seeds must have scattered into the air when Queen Malice made the wind blow us out of the Secret Garden,"

"How wonderful! My dear friends,

I can't thank you enough," the little king said. "If my sister had had her way the kingdom would be covered with weeds and horrible snap traps, but instead it will be as beautiful as ever. Every time I see a flower I shall think of you and be very, very glad that the Magic Box brought me three special – and important – friends."

Summer gave him a hug. "And every time we see a flower we'll think of the Secret Kingdom, King Merry. We love coming here!"

"Can we come back and see the kingdom when all the new flowers have bloomed?" Ellie asked eagerly.

King Merry smiled. "Of course, my dear. But for now, it is time for you to return home."

"We'll see you again very soon," promised Trixi. She flew her leaf up to kiss the very tips of their noses.

"Bye, Trixi. Bye, King Merry," they all said. It was sad to be leaving the Secret Kingdom, but they knew they would be back for more adventures soon.

Trixi tapped her ring and a cloud of pink flower petals swirled around the girls, sweeping them away. Summer, Jasmine and Ellie tumbled over and over until they came to a stop. They blinked their eyes open to see that they were back behind the tree in Jasmine's garden. The Magic Box was on the ground in front of them. Its lid was shut and it was no longer shining.

"We're back," Jasmine said with a wistful sigh.

Ellie nodded and picked up the Magic Box. "For now. But hopefully we'll visit the Secret Kingdom again very soon."

"Girls?" Jasmine's grandma called.

Jasmine looked round the tree. "We're just here, Nani!" she called, waving. Nani was sitting up on her sun-lounger, stretching. Ellie quickly put the box in her bag and they all went over to Nani.

"I think I must have fallen asleep,"

Nani said, smiling.

"We were just having a look round the garden," Jasmine said.

"It's really pretty," said Summer.

"It's certainly looking much better now. Thank you for all your hard work," Nani

said. "I hope you weren't bored."

The girls hid their grins. "Oh no, we *definitely* weren't bored," Ellie said.

"Gardening's never boring, Nani," said Jasmine. She winked at the others. "Especially in the Secret Kingdom!"

Join Ellie, Summer and Jasmine in their next Secret Kingdom adventure,

Fairy Charm

Read on for a sneak peek...

A Message From King Merry

Ellie Macdonald smiled as she put the finishing touches to her sketch of a pyramid. She and her best friends, Summer Hammond and Jasmine Smith, were in their classroom at Honeyvale School making a poster about Ancient Egypt as a class project. Next to Ellie, Jasmine was humming under her breath as she wrote out a list of different

Egyptian gods, and on the other side of Ellie, Summer was playing with the end of one of her blonde plaits as she looked through a book about Ancient Egypt. Around them, the rest of the class were working hard on their posters too.

"What do you think?" Ellie asked, showing Summer and Jasmine her picture.

"It's great," said Summer.

"It really is," Jasmine agreed. "Maybe you should draw a mummy next?"

"Sure." Ellie's green eyes sparkled. "Hey, what are a mummy's favourite flowers?"

"I don't know," said Summer.

Ellie grinned. "Chrysanthe*mummies*, of course!"

Jasmine and Summer groaned.

"That's awful, Ellie!" Jasmine said.

"I can think of some more jokes

if you like," said Ellie.

"No, save us." Jasmine pretended to plead.

"Summer giggled. "We'd better get on with this poster, you two," she said. "I think I might write something about the pyramids now. Did you know the Ancient Egyptians used to put traps inside them?"

"Why?" asked Ellie, intrigued.

"To stop thieves who tried to steal the treasure," said Summer.

"What sort of traps?" Jasmine asked.

"Well, sometimes they'd build a complicated maze so the thieves would get lost, or they might leave snakes in the tunnels, or build a concealed pit for the thieves to fall into."

"Oh, wow!" said Jasmine. "I'd love to

explore a pyramid. It would be a real adventure."

Summer shivered. "I'm not sure about the sound of all those traps…"

"Well, how about an adventure somewhere a bit more magical?" Ellie whispered with a smile.

Summer grinned back. "Definitely! Every adventure in the Secret Kingdom is fun."

The three friends exchanged happy looks. The Secret Kingdom was an enchanted land filled with magical creatures, and they were the only people who knew about it! They owned a wonderful magic box that had been made by King Merry, the jolly ruler of the kingdom. Whenever King Merry needed the girls' help he would send them a message using the box.

"Going to the Secret Kingdom is the most fun ever," said Jasmine.

Ellie nodded enthusiastically. "Even if we do usually have to deal with Queen Malice and her horrible Storm Sprites," she added.

Queen Malice was King Merry's wicked sister. She kept hatching plots to try and take over the kingdom. So far, Summer, Ellie and Jasmine had always managed to stop her.

"Oh, I wish we could go to the Secret Kingdom again," Jasmine said, longingly.

Ellie nodded. "I checked the Magic Box ten times yesterday, but there was no message."

Just then their teacher clapped her hands. "Time to pack away, everyone!"

The girls began to clear up. While Jasmine and Summer were putting away the textbooks, Ellie nipped into the cloakroom. Her school bag was hanging under her coat, and the Magic Box was inside it. She checked over her shoulder to make sure no one was watching and then undid the buckles. Would the Magic Box be shining at last, like it always did when King Merry sent them a message…?

But no. The carved wooden box wasn't glowing at all.

"No luck," she said, returning to the others. "There's no message yet."

Jasmine sighed. She really wished they could whizz off to the Secret Kingdom. They always had so much fun – whether they were having exciting adventures defeating Queen Malice or making new friends, or joining in with magical celebrations. It was the best place ever!

At breaktime, Summer, Ellie and Jasmine joined in a game of hopscotch with a few of their other friends in the playground. They took their bags with them and left them in a pile. Ellie was waiting for her turn at hopscotch when she glanced over and saw her bag was glowing faintly. She gasped.

Olivia, who was in front of her in the line, glanced at her. "What's the matter?"

"N-nothing," Ellie said quickly. "Gosh, look how fast Sasha's doing the hopscotch."

Olivia turned back to watch their other friend. Ellie turned quickly towards Jasmine and Summer, who were standing behind her. Using her eyes, she caught their attention and nodded meaningfully towards her bag. They saw the glow too. Summer's hand flew to her mouth.

"You know, I think I'll give hopscotch a miss this breaktime," Jasmine said loudly.

"Me too," said Ellie and Summer.

Read

Fairy Charm

to find out what happens next!

Secret Kingdom

Look out for the next sparkling series!

When the last grain of sand falls in Queen Malice's cursed hourglass, magic will be lost from the Secret Kingdom forever!
Can Ellie, Summer and Jasmine find all the Enchanted Objects and break the spell?

Secret Kingdom

Collect all the amazing Secret Kingdom specials - with two exciting adventures in one!

Spotty Bug Search

The spotty bugs need to collect more flowers! Can you help them find the way through the maze?

Secret Kingdom

Competition!

Would you like to win a Secret Kingdom goody bag?

Ellie, Summer and Jasmine love all the magical flowers in the Secret Garden. But there are still many more to discover. They would like you to create your own magical flower!

All you have to do is design your flower and tell us about its magical powers!

Send your flower in to us at
Secret Kingdom Petal Parade Competition
Orchard Books, 338 Euston Road, London, NW1 3BH

Two lucky winners will receive an extra special Secret Kingdom goody bag.

Don't forget to add your name and address.

Good luck!

Closing date:
30th November 2015

Competition open only to UK and Republic of Ireland residents. No purchase required. In order to enter the competition you must join the Secret Kingdom Club. For more details and full terms and conditions please see http://www.hachettechildrensdigital.co.uk/terms/

Secret Kingdom

Catch up on the very first books in the beautiful Secret Kingdom treasury!

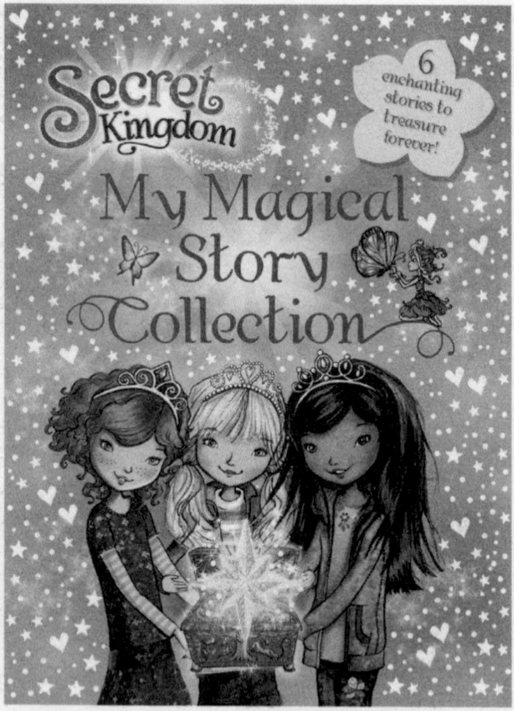

Contains all six adventures from series one, now with gorgeous colour illustrations!

Out now!

Secret Kingdom

Keep all your dreams and wishes safe in the Secret Kingdom Notebook!

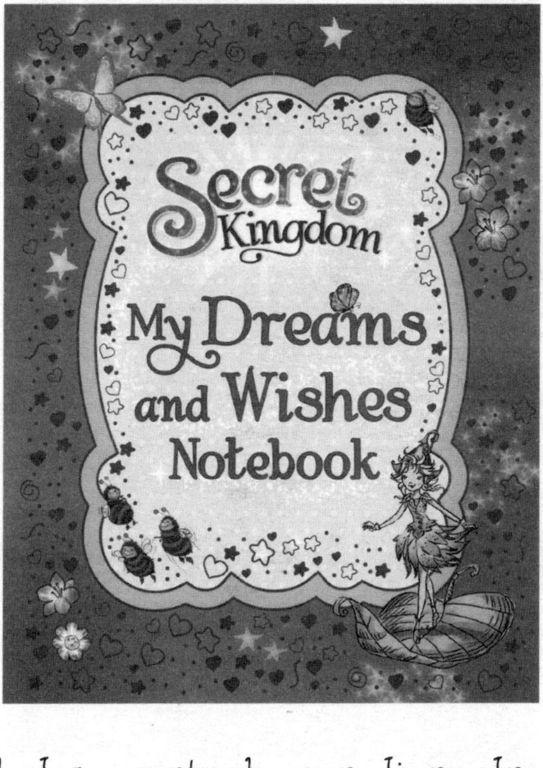

Includes a party planner, diary, dream journal and lots more!

Out now!

Secret Kingdom

A magical world of friendship and fun!

Join the Secret Kingdom Club at

www.secretkingdombooks.com

and enjoy games, sneak peeks and lots more!

You'll find great activities, competitions, stories and games, plus a special newsletter for Secret Kingdom friends!